To Mom

Rabén and Sjögren Bokförlag
www.raben.se

Translation copyright © 2001 by Rabén and Sjögren
All rights reserved
Distributed in Canada by Douglas and McIntyre Ltd.
Originally published in Sweden by Rabén and Sjögren Bokförlag
under the title **Gittan och grävargarna**
Text and illustrations copyright © 2000 by Pija Lindenbaum
Library of Congress catalog card number 2001 130144
Printed in Denmark
First American edition, 2001
ISBN 91-29-65395-9

Rabén & Sjögren Bokförlag is part of P. A. Norstedt & Söner
Publishing Group, established in 1823

BRIDGET
and the
Gray Wolves

Pija Lindenbaum
Translated by Kjersti Board

R&S
BOOKS

Stockholm New York London Adelaide Toronto

Bridget is the kind of child who never gets up
on the roof. I might fall down, lose my shoes,
she thinks.

"Come on up!" her friends shout. "It's really fun!
No kidding!"

"Watch this!" they shout as they throw themselves
down from the roof.

Here are Sonia and Robert. Everyone at the day care
center is going for a walk to the other side of the field.
They'll take along juice and cookies.

"We're going to have so much fun!" says Sonia.

Bridget gets to hold on to Nicky.
She gets to hold his hand for a little
while. Then he wants to pet a dog.

Bridget doesn't pet the dog.
He may have a splinter in his paw.
Or a headache. Then he might be
grouchy and bite me hard, she thinks.

Close to the forest there is a ditch with muddy water.
"Wow, look! A super-deep ravine!" the kids shout.
"Last one over is a rotten egg!"
But Bridget doesn't jump.
I might miss and scrape my knee. Or get wet,
she thinks.
"Now we are going to collect cool leaves," says
Robert when everyone is across.
"Oh, what fun!" says Sonia.

The children collect an old running shoe,
two candy wrappers, and a soggy newspaper.
Nicky finds a fat worm.
You shouldn't hold worms—they want to
crawl back into the soil, Bridget thinks.
"Who wants to check it out?" Nicky asks.
Definitely not Bridget.
That's the way she is. She is afraid of
most things.

Bridget looks for pretty leaves, just as Robert said.
She is so busy looking she doesn't notice that
the others have moved on.
Suddenly, she's all alone.
Help! Where did they go?
I'll stay here, she thinks. They'll probably
come back.
Bridget waits a long time.

Then she starts walking.
She is probably walking toward day care.
But, my, how tall the trees have become!
She is looking for Nicky's blue jacket.
She is listening for Sonia's "Oh, what fun!"
But all she can hear is the sounds of
the forest.
And the trees feel dangerous here.

Suddenly, little yellow lights appear between the tree trunks. And she can hear the gnashing of sharp teeth. It is the gray wolves, lurking behind the trees.

"Come on out!" Bridget shouts. "I am a child who has lost her day care."

"This is our forest," the wolves snarl. "Go and play in your own forest!"

"Don't you understand? I'm lost," Bridget answers.

Then they come closer on soft feet. Shaggy, and rather grumpy.

"Why do you walk around with your front paws in the air?" one of the wolves asks.

"What a disgusting pink nose," another complains.

"You don't look so good yourselves," Bridget says. "So there! Do you know the way to day care? Mommy is supposed to pick me up at four."

"No, we don't," the wolves reply.

"Then I'll stay here until they find me," says Bridget.

"Do you want me to play with you?"

"We don't play," the gray wolves say. "We lurk behind trees and snarl."

But Bridget picks up a spruce cone from the ground.
"Let's play Hi—Hello. I'm It," she says. "You have to run
as fast as you can, and I have to catch the cone. Get it?"
"Huh?" the wolves reply.
Bridget throws the cone up in the air, as high as she can.
"Go ahead—run!" she shouts.
But the wolves just stand there, staring.

And the cone falls straight into the mouth of one
of the wolves.
"No!" Bridget shouts. "I was supposed to grab it!"
The wolf coughs and sputters, but the cone is stuck.
"Promise never to do that again," Bridget says as she
removes the cone.

"Let's play something else," the wolves whine,
"something that isn't so dangerous."
"Chicken and wolf," Bridget cries. "That's fun! I'll be
the wolf, and you can be the chickens."
Bridget tries very hard to explain the game. But when
gray wolves don't understand something, they just
fall over and play dead.
"Okay. Forget it," says Bridget. "You decide."

Then they are happy and shake their
ragged coats.
"We'll play hospital!" one of the wolves shouts.
"Yes, let's!" the others howl.

All the wolves want to be sick.
Bridget has to be both doctor and nurse.
The wolves flop down all over the place.
"In the hospital you have to lie in straight rows,"
Bridget says, "otherwise it looks sloppy."
Then they lie down in an orderly fashion.
Bridget has to go from one to the next and scratch
them between the ears or on the hind legs.
That's how you play hospital, according to the
gray wolves.
But Bridget realizes that all they actually want to
do is rest.

"Yes, yes!"

"That's enough," she says. "Let's climb trees!"

"Do we have to?" they whine.

"Ready, get set, go!" Bridget shouts. The spruce needles whirl among the trees as they climb.

"Good little doggies!" Bridget shouts.

"Now you may come down."

The wolves are not good at going backward,
so they stay in the trees.
Bridget tries to tempt them with blueberries.
But they are all afraid to come down.
Finally Bridget has to climb up herself and
help the wolves. Sitting too long in the top of
a spruce tree makes you feel kind of wobbly.

When Bridget has picked the spruce needles out
of her hair, she hears a terrible rumbling. It is
the wolves' stomachs, growling from hunger.
"I can make you some soup," Bridget says.
First she takes some mud. Then she stirs in
some spruce needles and a bit of moss.
She adds just enough water.
And on top she puts five
blueberries.
"This will be perfect! And very tasty,"
she says.

The wolves obediently open their mouths and
finish all the soup. Then they burp politely.

The wolves' forest is getting dark.
Bridget sees from their eyes that the wolves are getting sleepy.
It's probably time for them to go to bed.
"Off you go to bed!" she says. "It's nighttime."
"Noooo, noooo," the wolves complain.
"Yes it is," says Bridget. "If you hurry up, I'll sing you some
sad songs."
The wolves agree, because they love sad things.
"But first you have to go to the bathroom," says Bridget.
The wolves obediently go to their pee trees. And soon it sounds
as if it's raining in the forest.

The wolves settle down and make themselves comfortable.
Bridget is singing beautifully, as the moon rises:
"In a road, on a stone,
   sat a girl, all alone;
   shoes she had none,
   socks she had none,
   thin as a rail, all skin and bone . . . "

Large tears trickle down their furry cheeks.
But finally, one by one,
they all fall asleep.

Bridget is woken by an ant that is running around in her ear.
The moon has disappeared, and daylight is creeping in
between the tree trunks.
No one has found me, Bridget thinks. I guess I'll have to
find day care on my own.
"Bye," she whispers, and strokes the wolves' matted coats.
"I'm leaving."

When Bridget has been walking awhile, she hears a panting
sound behind her. It's the wolves galloping
on the moss.
"Hey!" they howl. "We'll come with you!
You shouldn't be walking alone in the forest.
And besides, we have nothing else to do."

Before long they are standing at the edge of the field.
On the other side, Bridget can see her day care.
"We're afraid to go any farther, "the gray wolves snarl.
"Will you come back sometime?"
"Maybe," says Bridget.
"If you do, we can play and make some soup,"
the wolves shout after her.

THE END

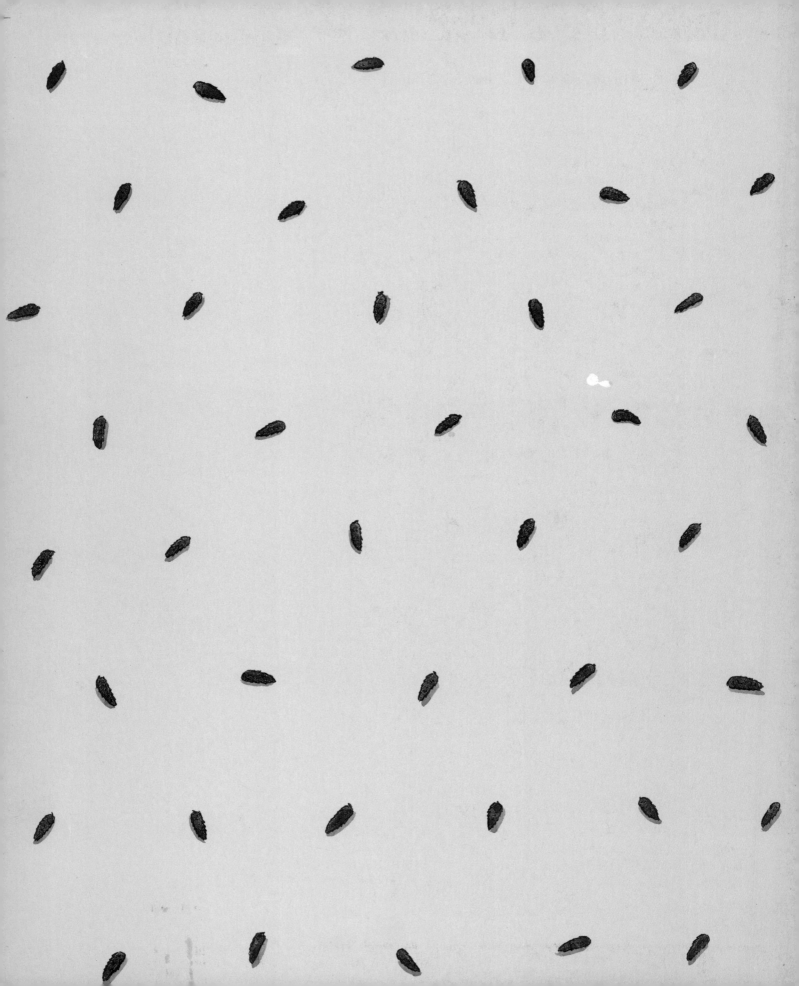